PRESENTED BY USA TODAY BESTSELLING AUTHOR

DANIEL ARTHUR SMITH

Tales from the Canyons of the Damned 39

First Edition

Special thanks to editor Jessica West

ISBN: 978-1-946777-95-9

Cover By Daniel Arthur Smith

Horror Fiction from Holt Smith ltd
Agroland
Tower
Attack of the Kung Fu Mummies

For Susan, Tristan, & Oliver, as all things are.

The Voodoo Queen
Steve Oden

VOODOO DOLL COVERED HER single, red-button eye with a stubby, fingerless hand while peering through the stitched X on the other side of her sack-like head. The crisscrossed letter hid an embedded lens with telescopic range-finding features, video capability, and UV sensor.

The automatic diaphragm clicked into focus. More than 2,000 meters distant, the blurry image resolved itself into a military convoy. One of the enemy's kingdoms was resupplying a forward outpost. Dust rose from the fans of ground-effect trucks guarded by lackadaisical teenaged soldiers.

The cowards would scream and run when the ambush kicked off. Several tons of food and ammunition wasn't worth dying for, especially when they saw the demons she intended to unleash. It wasn't the supplies or vehicles she wanted, however. Control of the outpost was her ultimate goal. She intended to take the position, fortify the perimeter, and hold the junction for its strategic value.

Soon, there would be a new player on the board. Her chess piece was in the shape of a black heart, just like the one raggedly sewn on her torso.

Magic and mayhem, those were the promises she'd make to the cruel kingdoms of children and adolescents. Their foes, the rebellious live and bio-mechanical toys, would find her even more implacable.

She transmitted the convoy's image to the flanking demon guerilla units hidden in ruins on both sides of the road. "Counting down now, from five, four, three…" she whispered in the throat microphone and speaker sewn behind the stitches of her frowning mouth.

The demons burst forth with a high keening, a nightmare assault that caught the armored gates swinging open for the vehicles.

Trained in close and silent combat, the demons used scythe-tipped appendages and dagger-shaped fangs to dispatch the hapless guard detail and overcome the outpost's surprised defenders.

Her orders were clear: Don't stop to feed. That would come later.

Voodoo Doll wanted the position overwhelmed before the humans had a chance to destroy the valuable field communication equipment, high-caliber armaments, and energy weapons. She coveted all of these, but the road junction itself was the greatest prize.

Feeding on the flesh and blood of victims was a reward for later. The rituals had to be observed, the dark spirits placated, and the demons taught to fear and revere her—for she intended to be more than a lumpy, crudely-crafted doll that hobbled when it walked.

Indeed, her goal was to declare herself the ruler of this battle-wrecked city. She would reign with terrible and vengeful cruelty in order to bring on a millennium even darker and more deadly than the past years of war. They would worship and serve her, the Voodoo Queen.

The screams of the garrison being slaughtered might have brought a smile if it wasn't for the tightness of her stitching.

The allied rebellion's supreme commander, Fuzzy Bear, paced inside the bunker of his headquarters deep in the ruins of what had once been an indoor stadium. Three steps one way, three back. Not much room to work off tension because the command center was crowded with staffers and their aides.

The blind bear hated his new title and the fact that he had to wear a uniform befitting his rank. A gaudy, formal thing, it made him the perfect target for snipers and assassins. He couldn't wait to change into fatigues, but first he needed to understand what the garbled radio messages meant.

His intelligence section, commanded by the Sikh toy elephant Brigadier Pachyderm, had intercepted chatter after an emergency call went out from one of the enemy's forward positions.

"Said they were under attack, suh."

Pachy unfurled his tattooed trunk and tapped a communication transcript.

"Other than occasional combat patrols, we have no assets in the area. This might be a feud between kingdoms. But my opinion is that after the coups by freedom fighters in Saxony and Little Beijing, the remaining city states are loathe to conduct internecine warfare."

Generational disputes recently flared between feudal monarchist young adults and the more free-thinking new adolescents. The latter wanted democratic rule and abolishment of slavery. The Chinese enclave and the Saxon state had fallen after brief but bloody civil conflicts.

Little Beijing had immediately allied itself to the rebellion, contributing a squadron of whirligig-fighters and three companies of rocket men. Saxony was in diplomatic talks with the rebellion, but the sticking point was how horse-mounted knights in old-fashioned armor would be integrated into rebel ground forces.

The slaves of both kingdoms had flocked to the Free Toys banner and were under its protection.

"Our contacts in Saxony and Beijing believe this is probably related to an outside aggressor, maybe one of the mercenary forces," Pachy continued.

A white-bearded man in a League of Free Elves uniform cleared his throat. Santos von Clauswitz, leader of the formidable death-elves brigade, stood to attention and asked, "Permission to speak, Supreme Commander?"

Bear winced. Santos, a formal and old-fashioned warrior, enjoyed addressing his leader with the proper honorifics. The blind teddy bear had spared the general's surviving mercenary fighting force after a battlefield defeat and invited them to join the allies.

He nodded at the grizzled human soldier.

"The mercenary units are hesitant to contract with the kingdoms after what happened at Barony Cadwaller," he said. "The outcome of civil wars in the other two kingdoms convinced the mercs that things are too unstable, plus it is risky dealing with those trumped-up teenaged royals, nobles, and their ignorant military leaders."

His single blue eyes settled on the bear's face with pride. "They also realize that the Free Toys have become a formidable fighting force, commanded by a tactician exceeding anyone on their payrolls. I mean that sincerely, sir!"

Saluting smartly, he took a step backward as the entire staff joined in applause.

The supreme commander sighed inwardly. "At ease, General. Your valuable information is noted. My gut tells me this is something different. Maybe an attempt to sow confusion in advance of a power struggle between the remaining enemy kingdoms."

The Free Toys had long benefited from the inability of their opponents to coordinate strategy and resources. Battles that the smaller, less well-armed rebels should have lost went the other way because of feuding, jealousy, and power struggles.

"My opinion is that someone is trying to consolidate the kingdoms under one flag. I am afraid their goal is to take over the independent fiefdoms, either through threats or by deposing existing rulers. This would be extremely bad for us and might extend the war for years."

A kerfuffle broke out around Pachy when communication technicians, whispering in agitation, pointed at the main monitor. "Commander, you should see this," said the turbaned intelligence officer, immediately embarrassed when other staffers laughed.

The blind bear smiled. "Never mind, describe it to me."

"Suh, one of our combat patrols intercepted a tight beam data packet apparently sent to all the kingdoms who oppose the Free Toys and our allies. It's audio and video. May I play it for you?"

"By all means."

A blurry image congealed on the screen. The face was misshapen, the body like a poorly stuffed toy. No hands or feet, only blunt appendages. Crude thread-stitched features seemed animated by rage. It was clearly alive but spoke in a tinny electronic voice.

"My army of demons now controls the crossroads through which your military assets must move to effectively assault the Free Toys," said the burlap face with one button-eye. The video camera panned to show nightmare creatures cannibalizing the bodies of young soldiers wearing the uniforms of Count Thaddeus's kingdom.

"It's a voodoo doll!" said Sock Puppet, his new XO since Toy Soldier had been promoted to command all ground operations in contested sectors.

Pachy instructed one of the techs to open a window on the monitor where the weird doll was frozen on the larger display. A digital map popped up, and the Sikh warrior clicked to enlarge it.

"Suh, we traced the source of the signal to this road junction. It is an outpost for Kingdom Thaddeus that we thought had no strategic importance."

"Show me on the battle board," urged the bear. The staff parted to open a path to a large model of the entire ravaged city and the lands around it. This was the way the blind supreme commander could "see" the terrain, road networks, bridges, tunnels, rivers, lakes and any ruins with potential tactical value.

Blunt but nimble claws danced across the board, finally locating the junction by using Pachy's verbal map directions. His hands stopped there. Although he couldn't see, the bear's muzzle lowered until it was only centimeters away from the battle board. His nose quivered, almost as if he smelled something.

"This outpost seems unimportant. However, the capitulation of Cadwaller Barony and the revolutions in

Little Beijing and Saxony—here, here and here—have changed the field of play!"

Bear thumped the board to drive home his point.

"What we assumed, from our perspective, were positive developments in fact restricted the remaining enemy kingdoms in their lines of possible attack against us. They must funnel their forces through this road junction in order to effectively mount an offensive."

The supreme commander wanted to smash his forehead on the board. He'd been so stupid not to recognize the importance of this small forward outpost.

"Whoever controls this chokepoint influences the war's outcome!" he said, then stopped to reach into a box full of game pieces in the shape of cannons, ships, tanks, and infantry.

Several new pieces had been added, and two of those the blind bear extracted and placed on the battle board. One was a winged dog. The other a rocket. His scarred face broadened in a smile.

"Get me our all-sector commander on a scrambled frequency. Everyone here, I want you to prepare unit dispositions and resource reports. My question is what can we throw together as a task force and how long to get it rolling?"

Sock Puppet's crepe fabric face revealed surprise. "Sir, what does this mean?"

Fuzzy Bear held up the dog and rocket board pieces and chuckled with satisfaction.

"It means we're going on the attack!"

Count Thaddeus, one of the most senior kingdom rulers at the ripe old age of nineteen, snorted at the video image of a living toy shaped like a sack with poorly stitched features.

"What, exactly, is that thing?"

His field marshal, a pimply-faced youth dressed in a garish uniform with epaulettes so heavy they made his shoulders sag, answered, "Apparently some type of homemade bio-mechanical. Definitely not genetically engineered. Probably one of a kind, sir."

"And those so-called demons?"

"We believe those to be lab-grown models similar to the goblin spawn engineered by the Halloween Kingdom before the Free Toys set off an EMP bomb that fried all their command-and-control technology. Very hardy on the battlefield, stealthy, murderous, and carnivorous. Without self-destruct brain implants, almost impossible to control unless they imprint on an alpha leader at an early age."

The count's valet lit a cigarette and handed it to him. He was known as a teetotaler who eschewed alcohol and drugs, worked out in the gymnasium daily, and ate no red meat. Tobacco was his vice.

"Estimated size of this demon force?"

The field marshal shook his head. "There can't be many, sir. Since the surprise attack, we've monitored the junction with drones and hidden robot recon units. They've beefed up a defense perimeter anchored on the outpost but haven't brought up heavy weaponry of any type," he said.

"Our best estimate indicates a regiment of the demons would be needed to hold the position against a superior force like we can bring to bear."

"And they don't comprise a regiment?"

The field marshal sneered. "Probably not more than a brigade."

"Against armor like our heavy tanks and a corps of robot soldiers, even a well-supported and heavily armed regiment wouldn't stand a chance," observed Count Thaddeus. He puffed his cheeks and exhaled a blue smoke ring scented of cloves. Then, he poked a hole in the ring with his riding crop.

"And the demons haven't found the tunnels we constructed?"

"Our cameras and security devices indicate no activity in the tunnels. If they discover the boreholes, automatic defense systems will activate to release poison gas and arm the flechette-dispersing anti-personnel mines planted every three meters in the floors and ceilings."

The count pondered for a moment. "I want constant intelligence monitoring of the situation and regular updates. In the meantime, alert our nearest forces to converge on the road junction and prepare to jump off at my command," he ordered.

"I also want the other kingdoms watched closely. If they have the slightest inkling of our plans to tunnel under the Free Toy defenses, they might attack us while our forces are concentrated in that direction," he said.

"This thing," he pointed at the doll on the screen, "has interjected itself in a carefully planned offensive months in the making. I want the demon fighters destroyed, but take the ugly sack of potatoes alive. I personally want to interrogate it!"

Tri-tracked tanks rumbled over the futile barricades of concrete and steel debris, firing pulse cannons at anything that moved. Moments earlier, a walking curtain of artillery fire had driven the demons to ground.

Dismembered bodies lay contorted in pools of greenish blood. Stealth didn't help when annihilation fell from the sky. High-explosive shells burst overhead, feeding a tornadic fire storm that scorched the rubble where the guerilla fighters hid.

Smart bomblets fired from heavy mortars became hornet swarms of death that zeroed in on the heat signatures of survivors. An entire company of enemy guerillas had been cut to pieces in their hiding place before a counterattack could be launched. Then came the armor, followed by lumbering mechanical assault units, to mop up.

The killer machines pirouetted on jointed legs like metal spiders, firing high-velocity automatic weapons and vomiting gouts of flame from domed heads. The AIs that rode onboard were implacable.

"It's a massacre, sir!" the field marshal proudly reported back to headquarters on a secure frequency. He rode atop an armored behemoth with a crenelated casement that revolved to fire a dozen self-loading missile launchers. The three-story mobile battery clumped on four flat titanium feet that crushed the already fractured pavement to dust.

The count's voice crackled over the speaker: "Have you captured the upstart leader yet?"

"No, sir. But I've assigned an assassin team to the job. They're working their way toward the triangulated source of the broadcast and report fanatic but spotty opposition. I can only assume they are closing in on the thing."

Unexpectedly, the massive weapons platform lurched to a stop. "Cease fire!" broadcast the mobile battery commander. "Someone's ahead. Looks like they want to parley."

Peering through the smoke of battle, the field marshal spotted a small figure standing alone in the rubble and looking up at them. A white rag tied to a piece of bent rebar steel waved feebly in the eddies of dust.

"Count Thaddeus, it's the sack thing. Looks like they want to surrender."

Pause. Then the voice crackled again. "Remember your orders, field marshal. Kill everything you find in and around the outpost. Bring the thing to me alive!"

He activated the loudspeaker and hailed the nightmarishly sewn creature in the rubble.

"Surrender yourself and any of your followers who might survive. You will be treated as a prisoner of war with all the protection and rights of military protocol. I am opening an access hatch, and you will approach slowly to be inspected. If you carry any weapons, drop them now!"

The curved doorway clanked open. Squads of the youthful marshal's guardsmen poured out to surround the doll. They were backed up by two mechanicals. The small fabric figure stood uncertainly for a moment, then took a painful step forward. Rocking to the other leg, it slowly advanced, bowlegged and awkward. The red-button eye was dull.

The dirty, stained burlap of its body ripped on a sharp piece of scrap metal. Revealed were the shiny metal and plastic parts inside, with lights flashing yellow and red in a rhythmic pattern. The guardsmen drew back.

The mechanicals swiveled their flamethrower nozzles.

The field marshal's mouth tried to shape the words of a curse. He had wanted to warn his men that the thing carried a suicide bomb, but it was too late. His reality winked out in a blossoming explosion when the mobile battery came apart.

Count Thaddeus yelled into his transmitter. There was no answer.

The hidden tunnels disgorged a horde of demon fighters: angry and hungry. The monsters threw themselves indiscriminately on the tanks and autonomous mech units. They carried thermal mines that melted through steel hulls, forming holes through which the ravening beasts entered and slaughtered the humans or tore the AIs out of the robots.

From video feeds broadcast by his retreating forces, the count saw a small fabric figure standing atop the smoking turret of a tank. It held a round object in blunt arms. "Enlarge that image!" he ordered, then wished he hadn't.

The burned and decapitated head of the field marshal looked back at him, eyeballs boiled in their sockets but still seeming to convey disbelief.

Rage consumed Thaddeus, and the desire for immediate revenge. However, military practicality reasserted itself. He was one of the oldest kingdom leaders still reigning, an ascetic who practiced emotional frugality and prided himself on self-control.

He never felt remorse about a decision, even if he had made a mistake. The field marshal had paid the price for faulty intelligence. They had learned from this disaster. Now was the time to plot the destruction of a foe who had ruined his carefully planned invasion of Free Toy territory.

"Order a fighting retreat. Tell the survivors to fall back to the river and try to draw as many of those demons with them as possible. I want the armored columns in reserve sent forward to form a defensive bulwark and guard the bridge at all costs."

He snarled at the scrambling generals and lower echelon officers: "I plan to maneuver around the flanks of these upstarts with two divisions and teach them a lesson that they won't live to remember!"

Voodoo Doll wasn't satisfied with her victory. The enemy had not been drawn in far enough, and the bulk of the mobile artillery and tanks she coveted was able to slip away. Count Thaddeus's forces now sniped at her demons from the ruins and walked curtains of mortar and howitzer fire back-and-forth on the tunnel access and egress points.

Every third round was a chemical-weapon shell. The pale-yellow mist was sucked into the tunnel ventilation shafts, killing more of her savages. They turned on one another, insanely biting and clawing until their hides split and bones liquified.

Contorted corpses clogged the subterranean staging areas. She soon would run out of fighters unless she could find a way to go on the attack.

The only strategy she could employ went against the guerilla tactics for which demons were trained. They would obey, of course. Especially now that they'd seen her die and be reborn through what they believed was black magic.

The Trojan Horse trick had fooled the count, too. In the eyes of her demons, she had become a goddess. They wanted to die for her.

True magic was mathematical. It was all about numbers. In this case, she pondered how to keep enough of her force alive and potent in order to take and hold their objective: the bridge. It had to be captured intact, regardless of the cost.

Her reserves would have to be brought up for a head-on assault. She wagered that Count Thaddeus wouldn't order the bridge destroyed. It was the only crossing point for heavy equipment and supplies.

The blood-letting around the outpost had been a major but costly skirmish, a wasteful feeling-out of the opponent. She had misjudged the tenacity and firepower of well-equipped modern infantry supported by mobile artillery and tanks. Thaddeus's youthful troopers were the best any of the kingdoms had to offer.

There was no solution for the disparity between the demon horde's in-close fighting style and the foe's long-range, death-dealing capability. They would suffer terribly in order to close with the enemy. She knew it was the only way.

They also had little time left before the Free Toys spied an opportunity. Voodoo Doll knew the blind bear was already studying the situation and soon would figure out that his best strategy was to let the antagonists bleed themselves out.

Then, he'd throw his forces into the narrow corridor, pointed like an arrow toward the bridge.

She was ready to sacrifice her demons in the meat-grinder. Perhaps Count Thaddeus was not. The outcome of this skirmish would be decided at the river. Whoever controlled the bridge dictated the outcome.

The lopsided stitches of her mouth turned up on one side in what appeared to be a grimace. It was a smile, the best she could manage. Because with the bridge in her possession and the enemy hurled back across the river, Voodoo Doll would set her trap for the Free Toys.

Talk Box
Ernie Howard

THE WOMAN AT THE self-checkout stand was at least seventy and trying to look up the price of a single, solitary orange. Thomas glared at his watch then at the old woman, contemplating leaving his groceries in the line that had formed behind him. *I cut it too close,* he thought. He only got to talk to her once a week, and he needed to get home. The box didn't work unless he was there at exactly 1:13 p.m. The exact time Alex had left him alone. The exact time she'd died.

Thomas took one last look at the lady and left his cart in the middle of the aisle. No one said anything to him. If they had, he wouldn't have heard them. It was 12:56 p.m. He hoped he'd get there in time. Otherwise, he would have to wait a whole week to talk to his love.

Charly hadn't talked to Thomas in months, and it wasn't much of a talk when they did speak. Thomas more or less mumbled about how they were supposed to get rain or something even more mundane than that.

When Alex had still been alive, they could talk about anything. Alex had a talent when it came to making boring things seem interesting. They talked about deep things too. Like how Charly thought she'd never get married, or about her mom dying two years before and left her with a considerable estate. *You need to travel Charly.* Alex would say. *Do it while you're young. You can't just sit in that house all day and mope.* Alex was the big sister that she always wanted and needed. Charly liked to think that Alex had needed her as well in some sort of way. Thomas had been the brother she'd always needed too. He used to give her good advice and crack jokes. Now he was just some guy who showed up at his house at the same time every Wednesday. Any other day he showed up at his usual time when he got off of work.

Charly was worried about her friend.

The day Alex passed had been a sunny, warm Wednesday. Charly remembered feeling angry because the weather wasn't appropriate for her friend's death. *It should have been raining and horrible,* she thought. Alex was a pure and lovely soul, and her passing from such a horrible disease should have caused Armageddon. Cancer had tried to take Alex's beauty. It would have taken a lot more than cancer to diminish her beautiful friend. Alex's light shone from the inside out. The day she died, Charly thought her friend just looked bald and tired, but no less striking.

Alex had wanted to stay at home. The room was the only thing that cancer had drastically changed. Instead of Alex's easel, computer, and books taking up most of the space, a large hospital bed was the main focus now.

The hospice nurse smiled as Charly walked into the room. She tried to smile back but all she could muster was a half-hearted smirk for the lady. As the nurse brushed past, her hand came up and rested on Charly's shoulder. The young nurse looked into her eyes. Charly noticed that they didn't fit with her young face. They were eyes that were as old as the mountains. "She's been waiting for you, Charly."

The woman was gone before Charly could say anything. She looked to the foot of the bed and saw Thomas looking worse than his dying wife. His face was red and slack with sadness. Dark circles had taken up the area around both of his eyes, and his posture was that of a much older man. He looked up and gave an almost identical smirk that Charly had given the nurse.

"Charly." She could tell by her friend's voice that Alex was having trouble breathing even with the pure oxygen that coming from a small unit on the ground. An oxygen mask hung from her friend's chin.

Charly summoned all the effort she possessed and put what almost passed for a smile on her face.

"How's my big sis today?" Charly said.

Alex waved her hand in front of her face as if Charly's question stank. "I don't want to talk about that. I want to tell you about the beautiful dream I just had." Alex patted the side of the bed and Charly sat down gingerly, careful not to sit on a hose or a cord. She picked up Alex's hand and stopped herself from wincing at the dark bruise that took up most of her friend's hand. The IV needle had left the mark after piercing Alex's paper-thin skin. Charly couldn't believe how old Alex's hand looked, and she felt ashamed just for thinking it.

Thomas sat up a bit and moved in closer to his wife. "Tell us about your dream, baby." His voice was threatening a sob, but he was hanging on for all he was worth. And for that, Charly was grateful and proud.

Alex took a shallow breath. Her eyes looked up at the ceiling, unfocused. "I was in a meadow with long grass that tickled the sides of my legs. Everything was so vibrant and colorful. You guys, I felt so calm and happy. It was as if I were lighter than air. I bet if I would have tried to fly, I could have."

Both Charly and Thomas had tears running down the sides of their faces. Very slowly, Alex reached up and wiped their cheeks at the same time, then went back to describing the dream.

"I walked and felt no pain. The air was warm and mild, and I tilted my head back and took a deep breath without even coughing. It felt so good to fill my lungs that I closed my eyes. When I opened them, I was standing next to a gentle stream with the most crystal clear water I have ever seen. When I looked across the stream, there were these beings of light beckoning me to come with them. I wanted to go right then, but I had to come back to you guys and say goodbye."

Alex smiled and it filled Charly with hope and dread. Thomas started to sob, and Alex patted his hand.

"Oh, my sweet lady," Thomas said. The sobs made his shoulders shake. "When you get there, please send me a sign that you're okay."

Charly started to sob, and Alex patted her hand as well. She found it funny that her friend who was dying was comforting them.

"You know I will. I'll find a way, my love." Alex tilted her head back. Charly knew it was close. The grief hit her like a ton of bricks. She wasn't ready for her friend to no longer be there. Alex sighed through her smiling mouth one last time. No other air was inhaled after.

Thomas, over the coming months, withdrew from Charly. He acted as if they had barely been friends. One time, he'd even been downright rude to her when he'd been running up his front steps. Charly only wanted him to stop and talk. He'd told her he didn't have time for her and that he needed to get inside. That was when Charly realized that every Wednesday he came home at the same time. She thought of this as she watched Thomas fumble with his keys at his front door. She made up her mind to just go over there. Alex would have wanted her to. She couldn't sit idle and watch her friend slowly go into madness.

The walk across the street, a walk she'd done probably a thousand times, seemed daunting and long. Charly had to will herself to take each step. Some primal instinct was telling her to just turn around and go back to her house and mind her own damn business. *Thomas isn't my problem anymore,* she thought. *We are barely acquaintances these days.* Still, Charly put one foot in front of the other. She owed it to Alex.

She got to the front door and saw that it was open slightly. When Alex had been alive, Charly had never knocked. She'd always just walked right in. Their house had been like her second home. She pushed the door in and waited for her eyes to adjust to the dimness of the room She didn't know what was going on with Thomas, but she knew it wasn't good. The man looked like crap.

She remembered what Alex used to say when things looked bleak. *"Desperate times, call for desperate pizza delivery."* Charly wasn't quite sure what her friend had meant by this, but it had always made her laugh.

The front room was dark. Thomas had the blinds closed and had drawn the drapes over the windows. It made Charly sad to see because Alex had always kept them open. Her friend's house was always bright with sunshine during the day. The only light that she could see was the light coming from the open front door she was standing in, so Charly decided to leave it open.

She scanned the room as she stepped further into the house. It felt weird feeling scared in a house that she'd felt so comfortable in and liked more than her house only a year ago. Everything in this house, and the way Thomas acted, screamed scary.

Charly stepped into the hallway that led back to the master bedroom. She saw a light blue glow that almost seemed to seep from under the small gap in the bottom of the door. It looked like someone had left the TV on in a dark room. It was oddly attractive to Charly; something was pulling her forward even with her trepidation.

She tip-toed to the end of the hall and stood before the door, putting her hand on the smooth wood. She could hear the muffled voice of Thomas and an odd sound that resembled low guitar feedback. Her old friend sounded happy, and Charly smiled.

She raised her hand to knock on the door, but the sound stopped and the light under the door dimmed.

All at once, everything that she was doing felt wrong and Charly took a step back from the door. She contemplated waiting for Thomas to come out of the room, but something in her told her he would not be pleased if he came out of the room and saw her standing in the middle of his hallway. She turned and walked quickly down the hall and out the front door, closing it softly behind her.

Charly stopped on the last step in the front of the house. She wanted to talk to her friend but everything about her demeanor surely looked suspicious. She ran across the street and sat on her steps in hopes that Thomas would see her and at least say hi. She knew he would come back out soon. He always did on Wednesday because, she figured, he was going back to work. Thomas was as trusty as a watch these days.

His door opened about five minutes after Charly had sat down on her steps. Thomas stepped out of the door with a huge smile on his face. Charly hadn't seen the man smile in almost a year and it took her by surprise. For the first time in a long time, he looked across the street and waved at Charly. Not believing what she was seeing, Charly slowly raised her hand and waved back.

"Charly, I'm coming over. We have a lot to talk about," Thomas said. He closed his door behind him and didn't bother to lock it.

She tried to make the ends of her mouth go down, but she was finding it hard. Charly thought she was going to have to corner Thomas into talking once again, but right before her eyes, he was crossing the street.

His eyes had dark circles around them like he hadn't slept in a while. The smile on his face almost made her forget about how run-down he looked. He skipped up the walk to Charly's front steps, making her giggle.

"Hey, Thomas. Long time, never see or talk." She figured her best bet was to keep it playful as they'd done before.

Thomas put his hands up as if he were warding off Charly's words. "I know, I know. I've been horrible." His smile faltered for a second. "But once I'm done explaining myself, you'll know why I was acting like an ass." Thomas looked at the two chairs on Charly's front porch.

"Oh. Yeah. Come sit," Charly said.

She wiped off the leaves and dust that had accumulated on the chairs. Sitting on the porch and talking was something she'd done with Alex. She hadn't felt like sitting out on her porch for quite some time.

Thomas sat down before Charly had the other chair cleaned off.

"She's back, Charly." Thomas rubbed the scruff on his cheeks and rocked forward in the chair.

"Who's back, Thomas?" Charly knew who he was talking about, she just hoped she'd heard him wrong.

"Alex! Who else would I be talking about?" Thomas let out a laugh that was borderline manic and chills went up Charly's back.

Charly couldn't look at Thomas. She stared out at the road in front of her house. "Thomas, Alex is gone." She gripped her chair like she would fall out of it if she didn't hold on. "I think you should see someone."

Thomas turned towards Charly. His eyes looked feverish and lost, making Charly want to hug him. She was about to when he burst out laughing. It was a hysterical laugh, one that sounded overly jovial and desperate. Thomas stopped laughing as quickly as he started.

"Remember when I was trying to learn how to play the guitar?"

Charly nodded.

"Well, Alex bought me this guitar pedal called a Talk Box." He smiled and pinched the bridge of his nose. "Man… It's almost as if she knew what she was doing. Anyway, it's an effects pedal that echoes back what you just played. About three months ago, I decided to pick up the guitar again. I was depressed and wanted to just end everything. The pain of losing her had become too much."

Charly gasped. "Please, Thomas. If you ever feel like that again, promise, you'll come to talk to me."

Thomas smiled and patted Charly's hand. "I'm fine now. I'm great. I get to talk to my wife every week at exactly 1:13 p.m. on Wednesday. She speaks to me through the Talk Box." Thomas said the last part like he was talking about having a conversation with someone at the grocery store.

Charly couldn't remember a time when she had been so worried about someone. She paused and tried to think about her words before she said them. The last thing she wanted him to do was to get mad and leave after what he had just told her.

"Thomas, I…"

"I know you think I'm going crazy. Shit, I did too when it first happened. I thought the damn thing was broken and picking up a radio station. Then I heard Alex's voice." Tears ran down Thomas's cheeks. "I asked her if she was in the meadow, and she said yes. She'd found a way to let me know she was okay. Then she told me she could only talk once a week because it took so much energy. So, she chose the time she died to live again."

"Thomas, I'm worried about you. It is completely normal to have a breakdown."

"I'm not having a breakdown." Thomas's words came out through gritted teeth. Charly had never seen the man this mad about anything. It made her uneasy. She scanned left and right down the street, looking for anyone that might be out. There was no one.

"I'm sorry," he said. "Look, you don't have to believe me now. Next week you can come see. Alex wants to talk to you." Thomas's smile made Charly feel the chills again, but she smiled back. Whatever was happening made him happy, and that's all she wanted for her friend.

"Okay, Thomas, I'll come by next week."

"Come a minute or two early. I start to hear her at exactly 1:13 p.m. sharp." Thomas said it like they were planning a lunch date. Not talking to his dead wife.

He got up and stretched. "I can't wait for you to see." His face beamed with happiness and excitement. He squeezed Charly's shoulder then hopped down her front stairs. Charly watched Thomas cross the street and felt the dread that hung over her like a blanket. She needed to get her friend some help.

Wednesday came slowly. Every day Charly came home from work and stared across the street at Thomas's house. *I'll see how far gone he is and then act accordingly,* Charly thought. *I'll get him the help he needs.*

She loved and trusted Thomas, and she knew in her heart of hearts he'd never do anything to harm her, but her mother hadn't raised a fool. She always taught her to be prepared for anything. Last year, she'd bought a long pocketknife when she had decided she wanted to try whittling. It would have to be protection enough. Just thinking about it made her feel like she was betraying Alex in some way, but she didn't remove it from her back pocket.

It was 1:11 p.m. when she crossed the street. She hadn't seen Thomas leave or come back from anywhere all day. Charly figured he must have stayed home from work. She saw the note on the door before she'd even walked up Thomas's front steps. *Come on in* was written in black marker on a piece of notebook paper, and Charly could see that the door was open slightly like before.

She pushed the door open. The front room was dark once again, but she could see regular light coming from down the hall.

"Charly, hurry up, the Talk Box is almost ready," Thomas said.

She walked to the beginning of the hallway and saw Thomas standing in the doorway of his and Alex's room. He had an excited expression on his face, along with a hint of irritability. "Come on, it's going to start."

"All right, I'm coming, I'm coming," Charly said. Seeing the excitement on Thomas's face made her relax a little.

When she got to the door, she stopped inside of the door frame and looked into the room. Thomas had the Talk Box hooked up to a small amplifier that was putting off an almost silent feedback sound that was getting louder by the second. Thomas's face had changed to something like crazy ecstasy.

"She's coming, Charly!"

Charly heard a pop from the amp then a voice she hadn't heard in almost a year.

"Hello, baby. Did you bring Charly?" the voice from the amp said.

Charly's eyes misted with tears. *He wasn't crazy,* she thought. The voice from the amp sounded exactly like Alex.

"I did. She's here, my love."

"Good."

The voice had changed. It sounded lower and guttural. Not Alex's sweet sing-song voice. As if Charly needed any more proof that this wasn't her friend, a blue mist came out of the amp and formed into a bright blue ball. Charly was mesmerized for a moment, until the mist started to form into a face.

The thing that materialized before her had long stringy hair, dark opal eyes that had no white around them, and a large gaping mouth full of tiny sharp teeth.

"I'm sorry, Charly, my love needed a body. Until now she hasn't had enough energy to come through. You were like a beacon of light for her. Now we can be together again. You understand, don't you?"

Charly's heart galloped in her chest and her guts felt heavy with betrayal. "Thomas, that's not Alex!" She had time to whimper before the thing flung itself at her face. The mist enveloped her nostrils and mouth. Some of the substance even disappeared into her ears. Charly fell to the floor. She scratched at her neck and face for a few seconds then lay perfectly still.

The thing that used to be Charly watched Thomas walk over to it. He looked odd to it. It studied the dark circles under Thomas's eyes and gazed at the muscles in his limbs. It reached the conclusion quickly that this was a human man of moderate strength. If it struck fast, it should be able to extinguish the human's life. The man's big blinking eyes looked down at it and the thing found its soft spot. The thing smiled up at Thomas. It watched as the man's eyes got big. The hope that the thing saw in them almost made it have pity for the poor dumb creature.

"My love? Alex? Are you there?"

The thing that used to be Charly reached behind the hosts back and grabbed the pocketknife from the back pocket of Charly's pants.

That's right, just a bit closer, it thought.

"Alex, my…"

The thing sunk the knife deep into Thomas's eye, all the way to the handle. It felt his bones crunch. One eye stared at it and the thing pushed the knife in farther. It twisted the knife and felt hard things mix with soft gelatinous things.

The thing looked down Charly's arm and into Thomas's one eye and felt nothing. It threw Thomas's lifeless body across the room and stood up.

The Charly thing looked down at the blood on its shirt, then at Thomas lying in the corner.

"Alex? Never heard of him."

Absolute Dark
Paul B. Kohler

I

THEY SAY WHEN YOU die in a dream, you die in actual life. Kind of like if you were to jump off a skyscraper and plummet to your death, you'd never reach pavement. And if you did, it'd be lights out.

Who are *they* to know this? If they personally experienced death in a dream, in theory, they would have also experienced it in actual life. Therefore, how would anyone know that they were dreaming about dying if they were no longer living to share the experience?

Or, did they experience someone else's death in their own dream, therefore extrapolating the cause of death while dreaming about someone else?

More dream research is needed to determine if one's own mortality is in jeopardy within the depths of their own sleep patterns.

II

When we lived on Earth, free time was usually spent outside, in nature; either hiking or on family picnics. Here on Vobos-3 life is much different.

I was between shifts working on the terraforming rig and was spending time with my daughter. Actually, I was hanging out in our hab, alone, and my daughter was up in her bunk—surfing Skynet, no doubt. And I know what most would say, but it's true, they actually do allow families on deep space missions, especially when terraforming new planets is the objective. Otherwise, the workers would go insane—much like my wife, Hannah, did more than two years ago. But I digress.

Like I said, I was on a bit of downtime and catching up on the news from home—news from Earth. I was relaxing on the gravity couch; an incredible device the scientists back home created to replicate the Earth's gravity here on Vobos. The gravity here is substantially less than that of Earth, and it's quite overwhelming because of its general lack of planetary motion.

Anyway, I was lying there in our hab ... and let me tell you, these units are like no other. They're not just tin cans scattered about the alien world. No, not at all. They tried to mimic our earthly surroundings as much as possible. You know, creature comforts from home.

For example, our hab has a living room, a kitchen, and a small dining area, all clustered on the main level. Up the steep ship ladder, there are two bedrooms and a bathroom. I know it sounds luxurious, but there's nothing grandiose about it. The spaces are really quite ... economical in their use of floor space.

So, there I was, lying on the grav couch, kiddo was upstairs trying to distance herself from her old man. I was drifting in and out of a catnap while the news was droning on in the background. I occasionally looked out the quadruple pane window at the arid landscape. And although the atmosphere outside was breathable, it wasn't quite up to human standards, yet. To limit our exposure to the environment, we were typically scheduled to work rather short shifts. No more than three hours at a time. It was three hours on and two hours off, to be precise. That cycle repeated three times per day, with 14 hours in between cycles. That was our 29-hour Vobian day.

It had been like that for the last 814 Vobian days, the equivalent of nearly three Earth years. But this day was turning out to be quite different.

Anyway, I was lying there, and I was staring outside, and in the distance the weather was … stark. No more than usual, to be honest, but there was something about the atmosphere that was peculiar. And when I say all of us wayfarers longed to see a blue sky, I'm not exaggerating one bit. The mustard yellow skies on this planet reminded me so much of baby vomit, it's not even funny. But today, that baby vomit sky was mixed with a nice eddy of milk chocolate swirls. Not only that, the activity was high. I mean, the atmosphere seemed like it was moving faster than commonly possible with our limited gravitational pull.

III

I dropped my feet to the floor and stood up a little too quickly. With our reduced gravity, I nearly vaulted myself to the ceiling. But my eyes never left the impending doom. The darkened cloud mixture was moving at a rapid pace now, and it was heading right toward us.

"Hey, kiddo, you see that out the front window?" I knew she wouldn't hear me right away; she probably had her earphones in. "Marie!"

I leaned my forehead against the glass and watched as several of the other colonists began to take notice of the cloud formation. Strangely, it was as if they were all frozen in their tracks, gawking at a disastrous train wreck rapidly approaching.

"What, dad?" Marie's rebellious tone echoed throughout our unit.

"Look out front. Do it now. Do you see it?"

I didn't wait for an answer.

Seeing as I was in between shifts, I still had my environmental suit on, just having unzipped the top portion. I quickly rezipped it and donned my helmet. I stepped into the vestibule and waited for Marie to catch up. "Are you coming?"

"Holy Hell, dad. What is it?" She nearly tumbled down the steps, but the lack of full gravity saved her from taking a header into the support beam.

"No idea, kiddo. Let's go take a look."

A moment later, Marie was standing by my side, also having jumped into her own enviro-suit. We moved out through the vestibule and into the gloom.

If you've ever stepped from the comfort of your own home and into a virtual tropical storm, you'd understand what it was like. The whirlwind, not two meters from our hab, nearly sucked us up. The other colonists from the surrounding units were all huddled together, trying to maintain some sort of mass grounding. Like that was going to work.

Marie and I joined the nearest cluster and stared up in disbelief. The ever-darkening clouds were lowering the ceiling height in the area. I felt as if I could reach up and touch the clouds. An obvious exaggeration, but the oddity of the situation was surreal.

Then, suddenly, it was like a tornado. A funnel dropped from the cloud and touched the ground. The cyclone began kicking up Vobian dust and debris about 30 meters away from where we were standing. The majority of the colonists around us were wearing their terraforming gear. Still, others like Marie, only had their light-duty enviro-suits on. No helmet, just a slightly thicker jumpsuit than one would typically wear inside their hab. With the debris flying around, my immediate concern was for everyone's safety.

"Marie, go grab your helmet and get the PVD. Do it quick." Thankfully, Marie did not need to be told twice as she ran back to our hab and disappeared through the port door. I returned my gaze toward the cyclone as it continued to bounce across the surface. It never really stayed down, touching the ground for any concernable amount of time. It just skipped along at a moderate pace.

"Jesus," I gasped. I spun around to see if Marie had returned yet, but only found that more of the colonists had left the comforts of their own units and joined the mass assembling outside. "This is not going to be good."

A few moments later, I felt the tug on my sleeve; Marie had returned. She did as I had asked and had donned her own helmet as she handed me the PVD.

PVD is short for Personal Video Device for all you Earthers. Each family grouping in the colonnade received one upon landing. It was part of our welcome kit. I guess they wanted us to document what life was like early on. We were the history makers, reluctant or otherwise. And well, this was something that was going to go down in history, I'm sure.

I took the PVD from Marie and flipped it on. As I started recording, the cyclone moved much closer. I had to zoom out to catch its entirety in one frame. It was moving so quickly that I could barely focus. In that horrifying moment, I noticed something that I was nearly certain none of the other colonists could see with their naked eye. This was no regular weather cyclone.

It was machine-like.

In the briefest of moments, I could see mechanical jaws open and consume a colonist before bouncing back up into the cloud. I gasped.

"Marie, get back to the hab. Do it now. Don't come out until it's gone."

"What is it, dad?" she asked, taking a few steps back. "You're scaring me."

"I don't know, but just get inside. And close the blast shutters once you're in."

Thankfully, she didn't dillydally. She ran with great urgency—more than I'd witnessed from her in a long time—and into our hab. I watched her every step just to make sure she followed my instructions. Being a single parent of a 15-year-old girl, you just never know what you're going to get.

By the time I refocused my sight on the monstrosity, it was nearly upon us. Thankfully, the mass of colonists had begun to disperse. I still had the PVD on, trying to focus as best I could, but the cyclone was moving at a frenzied pace. It just kept popping up into the air and then dropping down like it was dotting the ground. And with each poke, we lost another colonist. Hysteria spread quickly as the other colonists began to recognize what was actually happening: The cyclone was murdering our own population. I kept at it, though, trying to capture what was happening on the PVD.

As I watched in horror, I tried to second guess which direction it was going so I could get even closer. It looked like it was heading away from me and to the right, so I followed a few steps behind, continuing to adjust the zoom. Just as I got it dialed in, the cyclone dipped down, and just like before, a mechanical jaw opened and swallowed up Cliff, my shift supervisor, who I'd just had a meeting with, not two hours earlier. He was no more than five meters from me. And this time, before the jaw retracted into the swirling cyclone, I noticed something else.

There appeared to be some kind of eye on the front edge, just above the metallic mandible. It was quite humanlike as it articulated inside its socket. It was looking for its next victim. As soon as it locked its sight on someone else, the device retracted, and the cyclone moved toward the next casualty. And again, just like before, it dropped out of the cloud and consumed Veronica, Barney's wife, and lead civil engineer.

I'd decided then that I had enough footage of the disaster and began to put some distance between it and myself. I still left the PVD on, but I backstepped as best I could. Obviously, I did not want to stumble and fall. And that's when I saw it. The articulating eye stared right at me.

Jesus, I'm going to be next.

At that point, I turned and fully ran in the opposite direction. I was not going to let it get me. For the briefest moment, I was thankful for the reduced gravity of Vobos. The strain on my joints was far less than running on Earth. I was able to sprint much faster than I ever had before. I flipped the PVD to front mode to record my own face.

"Marie. If I don't make it back, know that I love you. I know since mom died, it's been tough with just you and I. Trust me, we both loved you more than anything in the world." I could barely keep it together as I recorded what may very well have been my last words to her.

I had no idea if I would need them or not, but I wanted to say something. There I was, running for my life from who-knows-what, this mechanical monster on this alien world. It was chasing me, and I could feel it getting closer. As I ran, I noticed the horrifying faces on the colonists that I whizzed by. They knew it was coming, coming for me. And they knew that there wasn't a damn thing that was going to save me. I felt utterly helpless in that moment.

I held the PVD out in front of me, and on the screen, I could see myself still being recorded. In the very short distance behind me, the spinning cloud was closing in. As if in slow motion, the mechanical jaw dropped out of the cyclone and came right for my head.

But, before it could consume me, I thrust the PVD toward the nearest colonist and yelled, "Take this! Get it to Mar—"

Darkness.

IV

"Marie."

Silence.

"Marie, I know you can hear me."

The low hum of the ion engines droned on, but otherwise, nothing but silence.

"Marie! Come sit down this instant," Hannah said as she nervously adjusted her own seat harness. "I can't believe you talked us into this, Scott." Hannah turned her attention to her husband.

Scott was intently studying the specifications of the terraforming reactor that he'd be building on Vobos-3. "Hmm?"

"Are you even listening to me?" Hannah waved her hand in front of his face, drawing his attention toward her.

"Oh, Hannah," Scott moaned. "I don't think you can lay this on me. It was your idea from the start. Besides, it's for the greater good. You know as well as I that without this outpost, Earth stands no chance against the Dominion. We made this decision as a family, including the heavy hand of your mother. If your dad had his way, we'd obviously be home right now, barbequing up some exotic meat he'd trapped in the wild."

Hannah's eyes narrowed as Marie finally floated into the seat next to her. "Thank you, sweetheart. Would you please fasten your safety harness? Commander Brooks will no doubt be by to check in on us."

Marie fumbled with the six-point harness as she fought to hold herself from floating away again. Zero-g's had its challenges. She giggled.

"Remember how I showed you, kiddo," Scott said as he demonstrated for what must've been the 10th time on their journey. "First, you hold the center buckle over your chest. Next, you take the middle strap on your right-hand side and fasten it in. Then, counterclockwise around your belly, fasten each and every one until you've made a full circle. The first two straps will hold you in place while you finish everything off."

Marie nearly rose to the ceiling before Hannah grabbed her leg and pulled her back down to the cushion of the seat. Once down, she followed her father's instructions and, one by one, attached each of the harness straps to the center clutch. Upon finishing, Marie looked up and smiled.

"Great job, kiddo." Scott winked and gave her a thumbs up.

"And there's that, too," Hannah continued. "All you want to do is be her best friend. Can't you be her father once in a while?"

"Jesus, Hannah. She's twelve years old. You don't have to overreact at every single thing that happens." Scott returned to his technical manual, barely able to focus on what was in front of him.

After some time, he closed the book and looked around the cabin. Across the aisle, Todd McBride, Scott's superior and lifelong friend, sat next to his wife, Darla. They were both fast asleep. In front of them and to the left sat another couple that Scott remembered seeing on the manifest but didn't know them personally. They were also asleep.

Once he was sure they would not be overheard, he spoke. "Hey, hon, you remember what the doctor said?" Scott chose his words carefully.

"I do. Your point?"

"Oh, Hannah. Even he agreed that it was probably a good thing for you, mentally, to get off Earth. A change of scenery was going to do you better than the medication that you've been taking. Isn't that worth something?"

Scott glanced over at Marie; she too was dozing off. Scott remembered that, as they approached the jump gate, the oxygen level in the cabin was going to thin slightly and, in turn, would cause drowsiness. He felt the pull of sleep inside his head.

Hannah sighed heavily. "I … I know. It's just so—" She paused and rubbed her temples gently. "It's just so fast. It seems like we just talked about going on this six-month mission, yesterday."

"You know it wasn't yesterday, Hannah. It was nearly a year ago when we signed up for this."

"But did we have to sell everything? I mean, couldn't we have put things in storage for when we return? We are returning, right?"

It was Scott's turn to sigh. "Yes, dear. We're going to return. But what if we like this ... this new life? What if being colonists on a new world is really what we're good at? It seems like nonsense to continue paying some kind of storage credit indefinitely, while we, I don't know, skip around the universe until we find where we really want to call home. It's just better this way.

"Is *that* what this is all about? Really?" Scott asked, fighting the urge to fall asleep. "Is it that all our possessions—"

Just then, the forward gangway hatch opened and in stepped Commander Brooks. Once inside, he closed the hatch just as abruptly. Scott paused their conversation for a moment as he analyzed Brooks' demeanor.

Commander Jason Brooks was a hard-nosed military man that Scott had dealings with in the past. He was not a man to cross, and he spoke truthfully. He was no-nonsense, and that was needed for this mission.

"Folks, we're approaching the jump gate. It's probably best that you all get some shut-eye. I know this is your first time going through, and it's not as pleasant of an experience as one might think. There's nothing to see out the port windows, and the entire experience leaves you quite queasy. Experience dictates that the exposure is far less invading when you're asleep. But again, the choice is yours how you want to experience it."

The commander spoke the words as he walked through the passenger cabin, glancing at each of the passengers—the future colonists of Vobos-3.

"How long will we be in the jump gate, commander?" Scott asked as Brooks walked by.

"From the point of entry here in this sector to the moment we come out in the Malfinio Expanse, it'll be about 90 minutes."

"That's it?" Hannah asked. "I thought our journey was going to take months."

"Cumulatively, yes. It is a four-month itinerary. Once we're out of the jump gate, we still have a few month's cruising time left." The commander appeared agitated at Hannah's questioning. "All of this should have been explained before we left. Did nobody talk to you?"

Hannah guffawed. "Oh, yes. I remember now. I'm sorry, commander. I'm just a little *off*, I guess. We'll be sure to get some shut-eye, as you suggest."

Commander Brooks nodded and continued his path through the cabin and out through the rear hatchway. As soon as the hasps were engaged, Scott spoke up.

"Hannah, have you already stopped taking your medication?"

Hannah ignored Scott's question. She eased her seat back, closed her eyes, and very nonchalantly brushed her chest against Scott's resting arm. "We must get some sleep, Scott. Commander's orders."

Scott chuckled and rested his hand on Hannah's thigh. "You really are too much sometimes, dear. Maybe that's why I love you so."

Hannah placed her hand on top of Scott's then leaned into him as they both drifted off to sleep.

The passenger cabins lights dimmed until all that was left was pure darkness.

V

Darkness.

I could say no more words before I was entirely consumed by the monstrosity's mammoth jaws. I did a quick check of my facilities and was surprised to find that I was in no pain. It appeared that none of my limbs were broken, or severed, for that matter.

As I tried to balance myself in my new alien surroundings, I was thrown hard against a metal surface. "So much for no broken bones," I mumbled as I heard a gruesome snap in my ribcage. And then came the pain. Without even a moment to catch my breath, I began tumbling in all directions, unsure which way was up. I tried to stabilize myself by thrusting my arms out to my sides until I made contact with what felt like curved walls. I tried to grasp a hold of something, but my hands came up empty. With no way of seeing, it felt as if I were encased in a large clothes dryer from back on Earth. Then it hit me. Or, was it that I hit the side with my helmet?

My helmet!

I reached up and turned the mounted headlight on. It flickered at first but then shone brightly. I found that I was in a circular steel shaft. Along one edge, there were metal bars, almost like rungs of a ladder. I wasn't sure how, but I somehow avoided grasping any one of them as I was spinning out of control. I was sure, however, that one of them was the culprit for my newly sustained injury, and I was shocked that I hadn't end up impaled on one of them. Not exactly being a God-fearing man, I moved on without gratitude and started climbing in what I thought was the up direction.

As I ascended, it was nearly impossible to keep myself from losing my grip, both figuratively and literally. The fresh pain in my chest did me no favors, either. The more I was jostled around, the more I was sure at least two or three of my ribs were broken.

After several dozen steps, I noticed that the rungs were coated in some kind of wetness. Upon closer inspection, it appeared to be blood, probably human. I stopped for a moment and looked back down. I could see flashes of daylight as the mechanical jaw again started up its motion, opening, and closing. It was hunting for its next victim. I looked ahead of me, or above me as it was, to see if I could find another person—it's previous victim—but nobody was in sight.

"Think." *What can I do?*

I was still wearing my terraforming suit when it hit me. "Wait, do I still have it?"

I fumbled through my pockets, and sure enough, I found a handful of detonators that I had been using earlier in the day.

"Jackpot."

By then, I had noticed the daylight from below had stopped its intermittent flashing. I was still being jostled around, but it appeared that either something was blocking the light from reaching me or the monstrosity had stopped feeding.

"Hello!" I yelled.

My voice merely echoed around me. The curved steel seemed to somehow deaden my tone. I tried again.

"Is anybody there!"

All I could hear was the whirring sound of the monstrosity, and a little bit of my own heartbeat pounding inside my chest.

Then, I heard it. It was faint at first, but as the seconds ticked by, I was sure what it was.

"S-Scott? Is that you?"

"Holy shit!" She's still alive.

VI

"Scott, is that you?" The voice was screaming now, and Scott could barely make out where it was coming from.

"Hannah, where are you? I can't find you." Scott continued climbing the metal stairway in near darkness. Having been assigned to the subterranean excavation division, being this high up in the reactor core was somewhat out of his comfort level. He didn't know what anything really was or where each of the blind corridors or stairways led to.

"I'm here. But be careful, the monsters are everywhere!"

What was she talking about? Scott wondered. He knew it was a bad idea to completely take her off her medication, but that argument was in the past.

As he reached the top of the stairway, he was faced with two decisions. First, step outside the conical structure and into the alien atmosphere. That wasn't an option. Second, he could walk across a narrow platform into the peak of the reactor core. "Jesus Christ. I'm not a fan of that option, either."

But Hannah's latest scream drove him forward without hesitation. He stepped out onto the steel gangway, his hands gripping tightly to the side rails as he inched himself out into the open air of the reactor. After several steps, he finally caught sight of Hannah. She was standing near the end of the platform, her back toward him.

"My God, Hannah! Get back from there! There's no railing in front of you, you could fall." Scott increased his pace but did not want to startle Hannah.

"I-I can't. I can't … make it stop! Scott, they're everywhere. Can't you see?"

"Slow down, Hannah," Scott begged. "What are you talking about? It's just you and I here."

Hannah's eyes enlarged far bigger than Scott had ever witnessed, and darted all around, not stopping to focus on any one thing.

"They're everywhere!" She hissed and then let out another gut-wrenching scream.

"Hush, hush baby," he said, hoping to soothe her. He tried to remember what the doctor back on Earth had told them about how to cope with her hallucinations if they were to come back. But in this situation, Scott only drew a blank. His mind was utterly overloaded by his surroundings. He stepped forward. "Honey, it's going to be okay. I won't let them get—"

"Don't patronize me!" she yelled. "You're just like everyone else. Why is it I'm the only one that can see these … these aliens? These alien monsters! They're everywhere." Hannah leaned out over the edge of the platform and looked straight down. From their height, Scott assumed that they were close to three-hundred meters above the floor surface below.

Having inched that much closer to Hannah, he could see the sweat covering her skin. And her hand, moist as it was, was barely holding on to the steel handrail. He knew that she could let go at any moment.

Scott took another cautious step forward, now only about two meters from Hannah. "Baby, I believe you. I can see them everywhere too. Just step back, and we can talk about how to make them go away." Scott prayed that his tactic would not backfire. Of course, he couldn't see the alien monsters that she'd been rambling on about for the better part of a month. He'd just chalked it up as playful banter because every time Hannah brought it up, she would giggle and laugh it off. He prayed to God that he could've seen the signs sooner.

"Y-you do? You see them? Do you see…" Hannah paused and turned to face Scott. She gazed passed him and onto the platform beyond. "Do, do you see that one right there, Scott? Tell me you see it."

Scott turned, looked, but there was nothing there. He took a deep breath and began to nod his head.

"Oh, that's not that scary. I see it, and it's—"

"You sonofabitch. You don't see it! All you can do is patronize me. You think that my medication levels are way off, I can read right through you, you bastard."

Before Scott could stop her, Hannah turned and stepped right up to the edge of the platform and was about to step off.

"Wait! Don't do it," Scott pleaded as he lunged for Hanna's arm.

Hannah fully stepped off the platform and began falling, but before her momentum took over, Scott grabbed her wrist as he fell to the platform surface.

The look on Hannah's face was of profound confusion. Then as the seconds ticked by, her eyes grew wide with terror. Full, unbridled terror.

"S-Scott! Get me up! Help me!"

Scott felt Hanna's sweat between his hand and her wrist, and he was beginning to lose his grip. "Baby, give me your other hand. Reach up, grab my—"

Before Hannah could react, her damp wrist slipped from Scott's hand, and she plummeted to her death.

"Scooooottt!"

VII

"Scott? That you?" Came a distant voice from below.

"Oh, Hannah!" I yelled.

"Uh, no, sir. You bump your head or somethin'? It's me, Mags."

My God, it got Maggie!

Maggie was an early colonist that refused to return to Earth after her last tour. She said that she loved the place and wouldn't return because this was her new home. And now Maggie was going to die.

"What the hell is going on?" she bellowed. I couldn't see her, but I could hear the fear in her voice.

"Hell if I know, Mags. Are you protected?"

I knew before the question was asked that she'd been decommissioned weeks ago, and that meant she was no longer wearing a company-sponsored environmental suit. But I hoped anyway.

"Um, no. I-I'm just wearing first clothes. Can you believe it?"

Jesus, first clothes were garments given to new colonists upon arrival to wear around our hab units until more suitable attire could be manufactured or provided. They were quite minimalistic and were not made to last for much longer than a few months. But some of us, including myself, and Maggie apparently, still wore them from time to time.

"Quick, climb up to me," I said. "I know it's difficult to see but feel around and you'll find a ladder along one of the sidewalls."

After a few moments, I started to hear the clanking of feet climbing the rungs. The sound echoed flatly through the tube. She was on her way, and as she came closer, my mind raced for a solution. I was holding on to the ladder rung with one hand, and in my other, I was holding one of the blasting caps. All the while, the metal tube we were in continued to shift and spin.

I had a flash. If I could just ignite one of the blasting caps, perhaps it could sever the tube from whatever this monstrosity was.

"Maggie! Are you close?"

"Yeah, I can see your light now. I'm almost there."

"Mags, no. Stay there and hold on to the ladder. I'm going to try something."

I removed the protective cover from the blasting cap and chucked it as far as I could above me. I heard it clank against the sidewall and waited.

And waited.

The 10-second timer seemed to take forever, and I wished I would've changed it to five before throwing it.

And I waited.

Four, three, two ... One.

Nothing.

Suddenly, something was pulling on my leg. I looked down, and there was Maggie.

"Jesus, you scared the crap out of me."

"You tried a blasting cap, didn't you?" she asked.

"Yeah, but something happened. I threw it up there, but it didn't go off."

Maggie was old-school. She had more knowledge about terraforming better than anyone I knew. I could only imagine what was going through her head at that very moment. She was probably devising a way for everything to happen just the way it should. She had an engineer's mind for sure.

"Maybe when you threw it, it bounced and switched off. Maybe if you set it and get away?"

"Not enough time. These new caps have a ten-second timer, and that's not near enough time to climb back down."

Just then, from far above, we heard the scream of what most likely was a previous victim.

"What the hell are we going to do, Mags?"

Maggie didn't say anything, but I felt her move up next to me. "Sorry, my friend. I know it's close quarters in here."

She continued to slide her body past and then above me. "I'm just trying to get by."

"Maggie, no. You don't know what it's going to do to you. That scream didn't sound good."

"Quick, hand me another one of your blasting caps."

I fished out another cap and handed it to her. "Maggie? What are you going to do?"

"I'm not sure what the hell this thing is, but I know I'm not going down without a fight. You have a daughter, Scott. I am alone. I'm an old woman living on an alien world, and I have nothing to lose. I'm going to take this blasting cap and shove it up its ass."

"Jesus, no, Maggie. We can figure this out."

From above, another scream.

"Not this time, Scott. Work your way back to the jaw and wait for the explosion. If everything goes right, I'll have severed this part of the monster and hopefully killed whatever is doing this."

Before I could protest, Maggie had already scampered out of sight. She was now in full darkness, and I wish I would've given her my helmet for at least sighting purposes.

As I climbed my way back down toward the metallic mandible, what appeared to be a trapdoor closed right below me. It was as if they knew what was going to happen. I looked up but could only see darkness. If I went back up, I'd risk injury from the explosion. I had to sit.

And wait.

VIII

"Thank you for waiting, Mr. Phillips. Commander McBride is just finishing up a telecall back to Earth. He should be done any moment," McBride's personal assistant Gary said as he tapped away at his communication display.

Scott remained seated at one of the dozen or so gravity chairs scattered around the cavernous administrative unit. Admin was one of the first to be established on Vobos-3, nearly 12 years previous. In comparison, it's quite similar to the colonists' habitation units but at a much grander scale.

Inside the main level resides all engineering disciplines, as well as reactor implementation. There was little doubt that the admin unit would be repurposed as a command center for the impending war against the Dominion. With all the digital displays already plastered upon nearly every surface, it would have been very ideal.

Various solar systems and orbital trajectories were laid out on half of the panels, while the others were detailing specifications of ongoing Vobos-3 projects. And although Scott had been in the admin unit numerous times, never was it for official business-like today. Besides Gary and himself, the room was empty, which Scott felt peculiar.

Then, without notice, a tall digital panel just to the right of where Scott sat slid horizontally and disappeared into a wall cavity. Behind it was another room that Scott never knew existed. He sat up and tried to peer in, but before he could catch a glimpse of anything, Commander Todd McBride walked through, and the door closed promptly.

"Hey, Scott. Glad you could make it. How are, um, have you been holding up?" McBride walked up to Scott and shook his outstretched hand. Scott and McBride went way back, all the way back to their college days. Despite the passing years, Scott still looked up to McBride as a superior, even a role model of sorts.

"I suppose I'm doing well, considering. Marie is your typical teenage girl. Her rebellious streak is just starting to form, and that's of concern." Both Scott and McBride chuckled.

"So, Scott. Have you considered my offer? I know it's only been a few weeks since … the ordeal, but our window is closing."

Scott began to pace around, attempting to analyze the nearest digital display. He did, in fact, make a decision, and it was one that he wasn't proud of. One of the last conversations that he had on Earth was with Hannah's parents, and he remembered the moment vividly. They'd made him promise to protect Hannah while off Earth. And he was damn scared to face them after what had happened.

"Scott?" McBride prodded.

"Yeah, about that. I think Marie and I are fine to stay on Vobos for another tour, if that's all right with you."

McBride stepped up next to Scott, staring at the same display and exhaled. "Scott, if that's what you want, I'll support it. But most everyone here, as well as those back on Earth think it's probably better for you and Marie to return. To head home. If you two don't leave within the next few days, you'll miss the window through the jump gate. You'll be fixed here for at least another eight months. Nothing can change that timeline."

Scott was well aware of the jump window as he'd gone through this process of decision-making numerous times before Hannah died.

"I think I'm okay with that," Scott said, turning to face McBride. "I just feel that I'm not through here, and if you could cut me a little slack, I'll be back up to speed in no time."

McBride's eyes widened, and a slight grin crept across his face. "On a selfish note, I'm happy to hear that, Scott. We have a long history, and I feel that I can guide you through whatever it is that you're dealing with. Quite honestly, it's Marie that I'm concerned ab—"

"Well, she's fine." Scott cut him short.

"Sure, she might be fine now, but what about when she starts really missing her mom, or distant family for that matter? At least back on Earth—"

"I get it, Todd. But we've talked about it, and our decision is set. We're staying. Talk to me again in eight months, and we'll see if our mood has changed."

McBride slapped Scott on his shoulder then pulled him in for a hug. "I'm here for you, man. Not just as your station commander but, you know, for whatever you need."

Scott returned the embrace and contemplated telling McBride how his dreams, or nightmares rather, have kept him up most nights since it happened. But he didn't want to give his friend any more reason to force him home. He'd just have to live with the screams in his mind.

Scott broke from the hug before it got awkward. "Thanks."

"Don't mention it. Really, we're understaffed as it is, and having you around for at least another cycle certainly relieves the pressure from back home. How about you take the next couple of weeks and just ease your way back into things. I won't expect anything monumental from you until you tell me you're ready. Deal?"

"Sounds good, Todd."

IX

After waiting a bit, I decided to be somewhat proactive about the situation. I'd noticed the cyclone monstrosity had started slowing its gyration. Seeing as I was not being knocked around like a ragdoll anymore, I switched my focus to the trapdoor below. Unless I could get it open, the odds of me surviving the ordeal were not significant.

I took an inventory of what I had in my environmental suit's pockets: I still had three more blasting caps, a sparging wrench, and half a dozen wire leads. I examined the trapdoor, but it was void of any fasteners. It was a smooth sheet-metal like substance that spanned from one side to the other of the cylindrical tube.

My first effort was to try and kick through. I gripped the lowest ladder rung and lifted myself up as far as my arms would allow. Then, I dropped as fast and hard as possible onto the trapdoor. I felt a small budge but not enough to make a difference. I tried this a few more times with the same result. Then I got the idea to possibly drive my wrench into the edge where the trapdoor met the sidewall. Amazingly enough, I was able to get the wrench's tip down into the crack a few centimeters, until I heard the next scream.

I froze and stared up. Obviously, it came from Maggie. *My God. It's too late.*

Abruptly, her screams stopped and were replaced with actual words. But they were spoken so far away I could barely make out what she was saying.

"Garble, garble *hold* garble *something* garble," and then it broke off. It was dead silent for the next thirty-seconds and then another horrendous scream.

"AHHHH!"

In mid-scream, the monstrosity began to move quite differently than it had up until then. The twisting and shaking that my aching body became accustomed to were replaced by a low rumble that practically vibrated the molars out of my mouth. Just as I thought the vibrations had reached their peak, they got worse. Far worse. I dropped my tools and placed my hands over my ears because the sound was so loud. Then, the vibrations just stopped.

Hesitantly, I pulled my hands from my ears and waited for a second or two before dropping my hands to my side.

That was one of those moments that I wished I wouldn't've reacted so quickly. The explosion that came was so earsplittingly loud, I could feel my ears begin to bleed. Literally. And then, just as suddenly, the entire monstrosity began revolting and spinning and shaking in all directions. Unfortunately, I could not grasp hold of anything to stabilize myself. I just had to ride it out.

At one point, the upward force drove me down onto the trapdoor so hard that I felt it begin to buckle. As I laid there, pinned to the metal plate, my darkness was interrupted when far above, shards of light began to creep into the metallic cylinder. At first, the light was faint, but it was there. Then, moment by moment, I could see the seams of the cylinder begin to split. It started from way up high and worked its way down toward where I was. After a while, I felt the pressure relieve a bit, and I was able to right myself and stand up. Just as I did so, the splitting metal tore all the way around and launched me out into the sky.

"Sonofabitch!"

It only took a moment for me to realize why I was feeling so much pressure on that trapdoor. It was because of the force caused by the monstrosity jutting up into the sky. I was now falling to the Vobian surface, nearly 500 meters below, if I had to guess.

As I plummeted, I could feel my heart beating, pounding ever harder. The wetness leaking from my ears spread across my face as the wind whipped by.

"Oh, Hannah. Baby, I'm coming to you," I declared, suddenly realizing the eerie similarities between her death and my own impending doom.

As I tried to maintain focus, my vision began to cloud over. I was going to lose consciousness, thankfully, before impacting onto the surface of Vobos-3.

"I love you, Marie. I wish—I wish I were a better father."

I repeated these words over and over, willing them into her mind. It was the only thing I could do to maintain any sense of awareness.

As I fell toward the rapidly approaching surface, I sensed more and more of my vision escape me. It was minor at first, but then it became so enveloping, all I could see was black.

At the moment just before impact, I was surrounded by absolute dark, and only silence could be heard.

X

At the moment of impact, I opened my eyes and stared up at the ceiling. I expected to see the mixture of baby vomit clouds but instead found Marie's face hovering over me.

"Dad? Dad, are you all right?" Marie said as she shook me.

"Wha, what happened?"

"You fell off the grav couch, again."

"Again?" I sat up and patted my chest out of instinct. The anticipated rib pain was nonexistent. "Again?"

Marie rolled her eyes. "I thought you'd gone back to work, and I came down to fix a snack. I found you thrashing around on the floor. Dad, you really scared me. Are you all right?"

I stood, rushed to the window, and stared out. "I, I must've been just having a bad dream or something." I rubbed the sleep from my eyes and turned toward Marie. "Has there been any weather changes today?"

Marie stepped up to the window and peered out. "Like what? It's been like this for, I don't know, since we got here all those years ago. It's just so ... drab."

"Tell me about it, kiddo." I chuckled. "Do you think we've overstayed our welcome? You think it's time for us to go home? Go back to Earth?"

I watched her and waited for a reaction. At first, there was nothing. But then it appeared that blood drained from her face. She backed up and sat down on the edge of the gravity couch.

"Dad, are you being serious right now?" Her eyes wide.

I sat down next to her, and she leaned her head on my shoulder. "I don't know, kiddo, but I think we might have gotten just about all we can from this place. With everything that we've gone through here, it might be time for us to move on."

We sat in silence for several minutes, neither one of us knowing quite what to say. As we sat there, my mind replayed various snippets of my dream. What did it mean? What did any of it mean?

Finally, I took a deep breath and asked, "Are you ready to hear about it?"

She didn't answer right away, but I could feel her tears begin to fall on my arm.

Her head nodded almost imperceptibly. "Yes. I think so."

I wrapped my arms around her and held her tight. "I was with your mom when she died. Here's what happened."

The End... Again

Jessica West

KIRSTEN COULD FEEL THE flesh in her most tender place tearing as the baby's head crowned. It took all of her strength and will to hold in the screams trying to claw their way out of her chest. If they found her here, her baby would be dead within minutes of its birth.

Kirsten's death would come soon either way.

While the contraction was at its peak, she pushed. Her legs trembled with the effort, but it wasn't enough to expel the baby. For one horrific moment, she imagined the umbilical cord as some sort of monstrous tentacle wrapping itself around her baby and dragging its little body back inside her. Almost as if she'd made it happen by thinking such thoughts, the contraction faded and the painful pressure and tearing eased.

She wept. Not from fear or pain or even relief. She wept at her own stupidity. Her baby would not die. Certainly not from any monster. The night of its conception, He promised her this baby would defeat the monster horde running rampant across the planet. They would not find her here. She would fulfill her end of the bargain and bring a saviour into this world alive.

Kirsten gasped at the onset of another contraction, took a deep breath, and pushed for all she was worth.

Lilith turned at the corner of Second and Holly Streets, and walked across the deserted parking lot of one of the few grocery stores that still had power. The generator sounded like a train. Surprisingly, there were no zombies. Maybe the only sounds that drew them were screams and such. Either way, a grocery store was probably a good idea.

"Smart girl," she muttered to herself. The surrogate had no doubt hidden herself away in the cooler. Good for keeping the smell from reaching the mindless, ravenous horde.

"No good for our baby boy, though." He would need warmth. Even an exceptional lad like himself would need a moment to acclimate to this new existence.

"I hope I'm not too late." She shifted into wolf form and scented the air. The unmistakable stench of blood and rotting flesh burned her nostrils.

Lilith growled low, deep in her throat. *That better not be His blood.*

Damien opened his eyes and shuddered. The world was a blur of shapes against a bright light, all encapsulated in a cold atmosphere. A flash of memory, from his father's days in the frozen lake of the Ninth Circle of Hell, jarred his mind at the same moment a pair of hands lifted him.

His arms flailed out at his sides of their own accord. He made his tiny hands into tight fists, gaining control of his limbs quickly but not quickly enough for his liking.

The pair of hands drew him closer to a face, all of which likely belonged to the surrogate. If she survived long enough for him to speak, he would thank her. Father was a stickler for manners.

The surrogate unbuttoned her flannel shirt and tucked him inside, wrapping him first with one side of the shirt then the other. She guided his mouth to her breast.

He didn't need the guidance, but it sometimes helped the surrogates to let them believe he was totally helpless. Until he fed, he was close enough to helpless. He was killable, anyway. The world didn't have time for him to die and repeat this whole grueling process. This time, humanity had taken their idiocy too far.

As he suckled, Damien sent out waves of soothing energy to the exhausted surrogate, hoping to lull her into sleep before truly feeding. Most of his surrogates died in their sleep. It was the humane way of doing this, and part of the agreement his Father had made with the human Father.

The surrogate drifted off, and Damien extended his tiny fangs into one of the large blue veins running across the top of her breast. As he drank deeply, a lifetime of her experiences—including knowledge of the zombie apocalypse currently threatening humanity—flooded his mind.

Her arms weakened as her pulse slowed and died. If it hadn't been for the shirt she'd so snugly wrapped him in, he'd have rolled right down her torso.

Damien took the opportunity to flex the muscles in his arms, legs, and back as much as he could. The scent of decay drifted to him. His keen senses could detect it despite the cold air. The distance was uncertain, though.

He could wait for them to find him here, and risk the mindless creatures not making it this far, or venture out of this cooler to meet them head-on. He'd have to open the door and desecrate the surrogate's corpse to lure the zombies to him. Damien was loathe to destroy the woman who brought him into the world. So he decided on a compromise between the two options.

He'd wait until they were closer, then he'd attack. In the meantime, he'd thank his surrogate by snuggling in close and napping in her arms.

Sudden silence and complete darkness woke Damien several hours later. His surrogate's arms, fallen to her sides as he slept, had gone cold and hard. The room itself still held a chill which caressed the exposed flesh of his left side from his shoulder down to his toes. The floor beneath his feet was frigid. The top of his head resting under her chin, and the right side of his body nestled against hers, were warm despite the coolness of her flesh.

Damien stood slowly, testing his newly grown muscles and bones.

The nauseating smell of rot threatened to overwhelm him. They were close. It seemed as though the mindless undead had found him after all.

He stretched and flexed, warming up for the fight to come.

Moans and guttural growls issued from outside the cooler. The sound of the generator had probably drawn them this close, but they'd never think to open a door and search in here.

Damien's eyes adjusted to the darkness. He opened the door slowly and quietly, but the horde jerked in his direction as if he'd fired a gun.

The isles were thick with them. Everywhere he looked, a line of zombies three and four wide filled the spaces between the row of coolers where he was born and the world of humans he was to save outside.

It always happened like this. The surrogate was supposed to buy him as much time as possible. He never grew past twenty years old. This time, judging by his height, it looked like he'd only made it to his early teens.

Lilith probably wouldn't make it in time to save him this time either.

With a deep sigh, Damien drew forth every ounce of demonic power his still growing body could muster. His teeth and nails elongated, as did his bones. A fierce roar burst from his lungs as pure dark energy filled his muscles. Power surged through his veins.

The horde sprang into action, pouring forth from the isles.

Damien sprinted to the nearest corner, to his left, slashing with his claws at any of the monstrosities that got close enough. If he could keep his back to this corner, maybe he could fight them off long enough for Lilith to arrive. Maybe he would survive this time. He had saved humanity enough times to have earned the right to live, right?

Hurry, Mother.

Tears streamed over Lilith's furry face as she sprinted toward the suddenly quiet and dark grocery store. *Please don't let me be too late.* She swore the last time that she would find a way to die with him if she failed to save him again. Demon or no, she could not keep watching her son die.

Mid-sprint, she shifted back into her human form, drawing forth all of her considerable demonic power and filling her heart with hungry rage. Lilith was moving far too fast to stop for the frozen automatic doors. She burst through the plate glass with nothing more than a low grunt.

Zombies took up every square inch of the store. For one horrible second, she thought maybe the surrogate hadn't hidden in the cooler after all. Maybe that was a dumb assumption on Lilith's part. Her precious Damien may already be dead. She missed a step and stumbled, sliding noisily across the polished floor and right into the backs of the mass of undead.

Lilith kicked and slashed as mindlessly as these creatures, fueled by intense hatred of all the things that had killed her beloved son every time humanity nearly wiped themselves out. She hated the humans most of all. If it weren't for them, none of this would be happening.

But then, if not for them, Damien never would have been born.

One of the undead bit a chunk of flesh out of her shoulder.

She shoved a clawed hand into his stomach and grabbed his intestines, ripping them out and flinging them as far behind her as she could. It wouldn't buy her much time, but the zombies closest to her would take the bait and give her a bit of breathing room. She snapped the neck of the disemboweled zombie and took a rapid survey of the scene before her.

Anger would only get her so far. She needed to focus. They couldn't kill her. Not forever. Not any more than they could kill Damien. Not permanently. But she could still die and repeat the cycle of rebirth. And so could he, again. And that, she could not bear.

Focus.

Lilith pinched her pointer fingers and thumbs together, then drew her hands apart. Between them, shimmering like a spider's web, was a line of dark energy.

This she flung out toward the crowd. The line severed all of the zombies within six feet of her, if the big red stickers at her feet were accurate. Some were decapitated. Some were chopped in two at chest-height. But all of them were dead for true now, their spines severed.

Unfortunately, the line was only about three feet wide. Zombies still surrounded her to her left and right.

She curled her hands and gathered balls of dark energy. With her left hand, she threw one flickering ball of what looked like black flame at the crowd to her left.

The crowd to her right jumped on her before she could unleash the ball in her right hand. She released her grip on it and let the energy find its own target as they fell on top of her, crushing her to the cold floor at her back. It would only take out one zombie, but she would kill as many as she could with her teeth if she had to before she succumbed to death.

She couldn't decide if it was worse to die before seeing him again or watching him die. Both were the kinds of pain a mother should never endure.

Damien hurled himself at the dog pile in the front of the store. *It can't end like this.* All these times she'd arrived too late to save him, only to either find his corpse or hold him as he died, all these times... This time, she made it in time to save him.

But could he save her?

He flung rotting corpses off of her, praying she was still alive. The irony of a demon—the Antichrist himself, no less—praying was not lost on him. But prayer was not reserved solely for humans. Nor was irony.

The corpses he threw against the walls burst like overripe fruit. One particularly vicious corpse lunged at his throat. He pulled back in time and swung his arm, intending to take its head off with one powerful blow. But the creature ducked back at the last second, then lunged again. The creature's teeth sank deep into his arm.

Her nostrils flared and she blinked in surprise, opening her mouth and releasing him.

He raised his arm, fully prepared to smash her head into the floor at her back.

"Damien?"

The son of Lucifer froze for a solid minute, inspecting every inch of her he could see. Aside from a huge chunk of flesh missing from her shoulder, all of her other injuries looked minor. That shoulder would heal quickly enough. She was covered in blood and gore, but he sensed no fatal wounds.

Neither of them had any life threatening injuries.

She gave him as thorough an inspection as he'd given her.

Damien helped her to her feet, and together they finished off the last of the horde threatening humanity this time.

They left the grocery store together without a word. Words would come later. For now, it was enough that they had both survived.

The Lost Tapes: Arrow Lake

Daniel Arthur Smith

"RECORDING BEGINS WITH TODAY'S date, March 24th, 2021. My name is Agent Melissa Muldoon. Present with me is Agent Lawrence Meyer. Commencing interview of Nathaniel Westerhausen regarding the disappearance of Hal Landon and his youngest son Peter Landon, neighbors of Mr. Westerhausen on Arrow Lake. Mr. Westerhausen, we were notified about the disappearance by the local police and we're here today at their invitation. I want to make it clear that we're here to listen and to help. I realize that this can be overwhelming, so if at any time you need a break, or anything at all, just say so."

"I appreciate that."

"Could you please state your name for the record?"

"It's Nathaniel Westerhausen. Everyone calls me Nate, though."

"Thank you, Mr. Westerhausen."

"You don't want to call me Nate?"

"Would it make you feel more comfortable?"

"I think it'll make us both feel more comfortable. I'm eighty-eight, Westerhausen has a lot of syllables, and I don't have that kind of time to waste. We'll be here all day."

"Okay. Nate. As I mentioned we're here with you today because the local police invited us to join the investigation. The reason we're interviewing you is because your selectman, Angus McConnell, said that you had something to share concerning the disappearance of Hal Landon and his ten-year-old son Peter."

"I do. I don't suppose ole Angus gave you a heads up?"

"A heads up?"

"Told you about…"

"About the creature?"

"Yeah. Did he tell you about the creature?"

"A little. We'd rather hear it from you, though."

"You don't think it's crazy?"

"Do you?"

"I suppose I would."

"Agent Meyer and I like to keep an open mind."

"This your first time visiting Arrow Lake?"

"Actually, Agent Meyer and I were here about a year ago."

"A year ago. Yeah. That family disappeared on the other side of the lake. The Mathesons."

"That's right."

"So this is a follow up to see if the two are related?"

"Are they?"

"Maybe they are. I don't know anything about the Matheson family. They were weekenders. I ran into Dennis a couple times. Didn't know him really. I know about my neighbor, though, Hal Landon."

"Then let's just focus on that."

"Of course. Can I ask you a question?"

"Sure."

"You probably think, in your two visits, that Arrow Lake is simple."

"Is that a question?"

"Call it an assumption. You see the people, the village, you think it's simple."

"I don't know. Rustic. Agent Meyer likes the fish fry."

"Well. A lot of city people that come up here think it's simple, and it is, but I've lived here my whole life, eighty-eight years, and I'll tell you, there's more to the Arrow Lake than meets the eye."

"Give me an example."

"I'll get to that. Let me tell you what happened with Hal."

"All right. So what happened with Hal?"

"A few days before Hal's boy disappeared, I ran into him at the transfer station."

"What day of the week was that?"

"Um. That was a Saturday. The transfer station is open Wednesdays and weekends."

"My mother used to say that's where my father went to meet with the neighbors."

"I guess that's true everywhere. That Saturday I was dropping off the rose hips I dead headed. Hal had the leaves he'd gathered."

"And did you and Hal speak to each other?"

"Yeah, yeah. That was the start of the whole thing. Hal was telling me that the pike in the lake were taking out the ducks."

"The pike were eating the ducks?"

"That's what he thought. He didn't see it himself. He said he'd been on the other side of the house cleaning up the fall leaves he'd left in the tree line. He'd had his boys, Sam and Peter, gathering sticks, but they're only thirteen and ten, so they'd only managed to make it ten minutes before they disappeared to the little beach. So he was raking leaves, listening to that political channel, the one with that governor's brother, and after a while he realized that the children had gone suspiciously silent. Which usually means they're up to some trouble."

"That's usually the case."

"Right. So he walked around the house to check on the children and he finds the two boys standing on the incline near the water, one behind the other, both with dead stares out onto the lake. They told him they'd seen the ducks being pulled under."

"Sounds traumatic."

"I suppose. Hal said they were more fascinated than anything else, started rattling out questions and telling him what they thought it was. He told them that it might've been a large pike but the younger son, Peter, he said that it was an octopus."

"An octopus in Arrow Lake?"

"Ha, ha. Yeah. Hal explained to him that it's a freshwater lake and that octopuses live in saltwater. But the younger one, he insisted he saw a tentacle. Neither of the children wanted to go back into the water."

"And what did you tell him?"

"I told him it'd be best to keep the boys out of the lake for a while and best not over think it."

"So was it a pike or a pickerel?"

"I told him I didn't think it was a pike, but Hal said that the pickerel were way too small to pull a duck under, much less a dachshund—"

"Dachshund? A dog disappeared as well?"

"Yeah. Mary Wilkes, Hal's neighbor, she lost her little wiener dog, Barry. That morning she told Hal that Barry was missing and that she'd last seen him near the lake.

Poor old guy was half blind, but he liked to swim. So to Hal's logic, ducks, a dachshund, it had to be pike."

"But you didn't think it was a pike?"

"No. No I didn't."

"What did you tell him it was?"

"I told him time to time there's something else in the lake."

"Something in the lake?"

"Beavers. Muskrats."

"Beavers and muskrats aren't going to pull down ducks. Maybe if they work together."

"No. Ha, ha. Hal said that too. But you know, a bobcat will pull a duck down, muskrat too, so why not a wiener dog. A lot of people don't realize big cats swim. Bobcats are the apex predator around here, you know."

"You thought it was a bobcat?"

"No. No I didn't. I just wanted the boys to stay out of the water without a ruckus, so that's what I told Hal. But it didn't make a difference."

"One of the boys did go back into the water."

"Or near it anyways. There's a tree over their little beach area, a red maple with a swing hanging from it. The young one, Peter, he likes to swing out over the water... Hal's wife said one minute the little guy was out there on the swing, the next he was gone, just disappeared. There were police diving teams, some local divers even helped out, but the body wasn't found."

"It says here they ran sonar, even dredged."

"Yeah. It's the brown water. The divers could only see so far in front of them, a yard or two maybe. Didn't matter, though, there's an underground river that runs beneath the lake."

"Underground river? Ah. Yes. It says right here that the diving team's sonar picked up a series of hollows."

"That's why they couldn't find the boy, or anyone else years past. When I was young it was just assumed that the lake, like many spring fed lakes, had a deep well in it, too deep to measure at the time. But on occasion, things lost in Arrow Lake would show up in one of the smaller neighboring lakes. They did a geological study and ran some deep-water dye experiment. Those hollows lead to vast caverns deep below the lake. They never found the boy, but there was little hope they would. I stopped in to check on Hal, found him sitting there gazing out his bay window. Hal had spent the three days staring at that lake, didn't sleep, probably didn't eat anything either, just kept staring."

"The report states he was under duress. Quite understandable. It also states that his wife Lydia took the older boy Sam to her parents. Leaving him alone—"

"Alone to stare into the abyss."

"You mean that in metaphor."

"Huh. The metaphor fits too. But no. I was referring to the fog that set in a day after the young one disappeared. Came in heavy, settling in from the coast. And there he was, no sleep, staring into it... I suppose the maxim has some merit—stare into the mist, it stares back. Because he was sure he saw something."

"What did he see?"

"Hal said he saw tentacles. Slithering around out there in the mist above the lake."

"Tentacles? Like the young one had said."

"Yeah. I told him that he'd been hallucinating. That he was seeing things out in the lake that just weren't there, seeing what he wanted see."

"But you knew better?"

"I did. I knew he saw something."

"What did you think Hal really saw out there in the mist?"

"Something. Something old. Something that comes around every forty years or so. I've seen it. Glimpses of it anyway. The tentacles, as long as a tree is high, slipping through the mist. It came when I was a boy, seven or eight. First a few animals went missing. Pets. The neighbor's dog, one of the goats the Jensens used to keep. Then people started disappearing. One after another, three in all, over the course of spring. No bodies, no nothing, gone without a clue. People were scared. My grandparents said that it, whatever it was, had been there since before the time of the Indians and that it woke on a cycle, every forty years or so. They told me to stay away from the lake, but I snuck down there. Saw the tentacles reflecting the silver of the moon, a knotted nest of them boiling the water, writhing in a slime in and around each other. I was scared stiff. Nightmares for years. But they were gone right after, and time went on without another disappearance… then sure enough, when I was late in my forties, pets started disappearing again. That spring I saw the water boil again, and that spring three more people went missing without a trace. That was forty years ago. Makes sense that it's back now."

"That many tentacles, could it be there's more than one? A hive waking like cicadas?"

"Could be. But in its presence, it feels…massive…and ancient. A magnitude of dark, suffocating evil. And there's something else. Did you notice any sadness when you got to the lake?"

"Well, a number of people were quite upset about the missing boy."

"No. I mean, inside of you. An empty ache, like there's a hole deep in your belly?"

"Now that you mention it, I have been distracted—but by nothing in particular."

"Exactly. Just feeling, a woeful feeling. See, when it comes, the whole of the lake sets with a sullen melancholy. And the closer you are, the deeper the ache. I felt it when I was a boy, again forty years ago, and I feel it now. The feeling of doom."

"Hrm. Excuse me. Um. Did you tell Hal Landon what you knew about the tentacles?"

"Not then. Not initially. I thought it best to cool him out. He hadn't slept, he wasn't thinking clear. But it didn't matter. He persisted. And against my advice, he decided to go looking for the creature."

"Alone? Is that the last time you saw him?"

"No. I wish it was. There wasn't anything I was going to say to keep him from going out into the fog, and when I realized trying to talk him out of it was as useless as talking Ahab out of searching for the mighty white whale, I came clean."

"You told him everything?"

"I told him what I knew, what I thought was out there. Told him again that there was no use even attempting to go up in front of that thing, but if he insisted, I'd go with him, on the condition he'd let me feed him and that we'd start fresh after he'd had some sleep. He agreed to eat and nap but he wanted me to wake him at midnight so we could go under the rise of the full moon... I was thinking that if I pushed him a day, he might catch his head. I'd brought a casserole with me and there was already a bunch of roasts and such in his icebox that the other neighbors had sent over. So, I heated up a plate and filled his belly. He passed out right there on the sofa, so I threw a blanket over him and headed back to my place to get some supplies, just in case."

"In case he woke up at midnight."

"Yes and no. I was thinking that after being up for so long, he might sleep for the next two days and by then it'd be too late to go out on the lake looking for that thing. But I wanted to make a good show of it when he did wake up, so I grabbed a couple of old iron trident fishing spears I had in the garage—they're seven-foot long—grabbed a speargun, an LED lantern, and my Winchester. Then I took all of that back to Hal's and sat there with him. I planned to move on to the guest room after a bit, but I fell asleep in the cushioned armchair, and next thing I know he's waking me up—it's half past eleven and there he is, bright and spry. I remember it was half past, because Hal's wife Lydia has three clockfaces there in the den. At any rate, like I said, when I woke up, he was spry and raring to go. I showed him what I brought, he added his handgun to the mix, and we took it down to the row boat."

"What kind of handgun was it?"

"I don't know the brand, Ruger maybe. Hal said it was a nine-millimeter. Anyway, by that time it was pretty bright out. I'm not saying you could read by the moonlight, but you could certainly see words on the page. The moon was full and the fog blanketing the lake was all lit up silver. The battery to the boat's electric motor was on the charger, so after we hauled the gear down, Hal had to run back for that while I stayed to stow everything. We had the two lanterns with us—both the LED kind with the white light—I hung one on a stick from the bow and put the other on the seat, but they were hurting the night vision rather than helping it, so I turned them off… Funny. In the moment, with hustling everything down there, the adrenalin and all, I kind of forgot about what we were doing there in the first place, but once I got everything stowed, and was just waiting there by myself, I heard the waves start to slosh up on the bank and that sick feeling I'd been carrying around became real intense, real quick. I mean, Hal couldn't have taken no more than three or four minutes running back to the garage, but time all but stopped. The water had been still, the waves were from something behind the fog, a wake, from something in the water. They grew in strength so that the aft of the boat started to rock, and the harder it rocked, the greater the dread, the hopelessness. I about lost my dinner when the waves abruptly stopped and the boat settled. Then Hal was there, dropping the battery into the back."

"Did you tell him? About the disturbance in the water?"

"No. I don't know why not. I guess I was in disbelief. Shock maybe. I mean I couldn't really believe we were getting into a ten-foot rowboat and heading out to find that thing. Everything in me was telling me we should be running in the opposite direction. But I didn't want him going out there alone."

"What was his state of mind?"

"Oh, he was giddy. Anxious. After we pushed away, he was leaning heavy from the till out into the fog, a look on his face like he was going to see his boy any minute."

"Not the monster?"

"No. It's clear to me now he was expecting we'd find his son. I suppose... I suppose he'd lost it already. And I was just seduced by his madness. Going out there with him somehow made sense at the time."

"But you did find it, didn't you?"

"Yeah. Or it found us. We must have made it pert near the center of the lake, the motor gently buzzing along, the mist wetting our faces as we passed through it. Out over the water that big full moon hung low and large, so close you could touch it—we could have been trolling a cloud. Then came the shadows. Fist sized dark spots moving all around us just behind the surface of the mist, so you could see them pass but not make out what they were. Then something a little more solid, a little more silver, like the back of a porpoise but long and thin, raced by the boat, disturbing the water, like the way a shark's dorsal cuts through the water, but closer to the surface like a snake... Hal stopped the motor, and the shadows continued to pass by, flying up over our heads, all around the boat, not circling, but we were in the midst, same with whatever was in the water. I could see the silver backs break the surface on both sides, creating enough wake to start us gently rocking. I picked up the Winchester, but Hal... Hal cried out for his son. *'Peter,'* he said in a whisper. *'Peter, we're here for you.'* I shushed him, to shut him up, but he persisted. *'Peter, Peter...'* Then that feeling again, that dread, it came back full on, and maybe that was good, because the look on Hal's face changed. There was no doubt he felt it too and was starting to snap out of his delusion of finding Peter out there, and when the first of those shadows buzzing the boat veered close enough to reveal itself, he was awake."

"Revealed itself?"

"To be a tentacle, upright like a cobra, silver skinned, the size of a light post. Hal's demeaner changed tout sweet. He called it a son-of-a-bitch, grabbed one of the seven-foot iron tridents we brought along, and swung it up, almost hitting me with the barbs in the process. The tentacle was wriggling around, the tip dipping and dangling overhead, probing maybe, just kind of hanging in the air over the edge of the boat, close enough to see the suckers. Hal poked up at it with the spear, but with being in a boat and the tentacle moving to and fro, his first attempts to stab it were clumsy, and rather than connect with the point, he ended up slapping the steel rod against it. And it reacted immediately on contact. Another tentacle flew up close to the first. Then another. See, I figure it wasn't the sound of him calling out for Peter that had attracted them, but a tactile alert, first of the boat in the water, and then the slap of that iron spear, and when Hal finally did harpoon one of those tentacles, we had the creature's full attention."

"What happened?"

"Well, all we were seeing were the tips of those tentacles, all three stretched up out of the water, growing from the size of light posts to telephone poles. Then the boat itself was thrust upward and we found ourselves on a sea of them. It was as if we were in the center of a lake of silver trees—not a hive, but one giant tentacled monster, the arms, twenty, thirty, forty feet long, writhing all around us in every direction... In my memory, the image, it's ah...spectacular, beautiful even, but at the time, it was terrifying. I was...frozen in horror. You see, when the boat was thrust up, I'd slipped back off the bench seat into the cradle of the bow. I tucked snug on my back, legs up, just holding the Winchester out from my waist as the boat rocked forward-back, side-to-side. And it wasn't just the horror, but the dread, hopelessness, I lost all will to fight. To move at all. Huh. I didn't realize it right then, but I wet myself."

"And Hal Landon? Was he frozen too?"

"Oh no sirree. Hal was raging. He seemed to be immune to the dread. I suppose, grieving for Peter, he'd used up all his sadness—no, not used up—become accustomed to it. The whole time I was paralyzed with fear, Hal was there battling the beast. Stabbing at those long silver tentacles as they swung down toward him, dodging, stabbing, kicking them away. It was futile really, swinging at the two or three tentacles near his end of the boat while we were suspended and surrounded by who knows how many others, too many to count. But he was relentless, relentless as Don Quixote. He got some whacks in, lost one of the tridents then went at it with the other, but…"

"But?"

"But… Hurting that thing. Stopping it. It was never going to happen. I'm glad he had his chance to scream at the beast. I'm sure it was much more of a stand than little Peter or any of its other victims ever had. But like I said, it was futile from the beginning. It all ended rather quick really. As if the beast had tired of him, or maybe it really did take a few swings to home in on him, because as soon as one of those long arms came in contact with him, two others followed. The first grabbed his leg, and he got maybe two stabs into it before the next two had slithered around his torso. Then they just pulled him from the boat, and they all disappeared. The boat dropped like a rock, slammed into the water. And I just stayed there, huddled in the bow, the Winchester in my hands."

"Mr. Westerhausen, Nate, Angus told us that you stayed in the boat all night."

"And into a good part of the next day. I figured that the reason the creature attacked Hal was because he was moving, the tactile thing, I figured, it must be blind. So I didn't move a muscle, couldn't have if I wanted to. I waited for a wind to pick up and send the boat drifting to shore, and me with it. Fortunately, it did, or I might still be out there."

"The report stated that you were the one to come forward to report Hal's disappearance."

"I reported what happened. They called it a disappearance. I believe they're still out there, combing the lake."

"Angus says that they're waiting for the fog to lift, it's supposed to as early as later today, or tomorrow."

"They won't find anything."

"I don't suppose they will. Not if there's an underground river that washes everything away."

"You know, that must be where it goes. Down to some deep lair to sleep for forty years."

"It's an interesting theory. One that makes sense."

"You don't believe me, do ya?"

"Nate, I told you when we sat down, we're here to listen, and to help. That means we're not here to judge you or any anything you share with us today. The sole purpose of this interview is to gather information in aid of the of the investigation of the disappearance of Hal Landon and his ten-year-old son Peter."

"But you must think I'm crazy. I'm not, I assure you. There's something down there."

"Mr. Westerhausen, I understand your frustration, but surely it has occurred to you, that short of the discovery of a new technology that can allow a diver or a camera down into an underground river that deep, or a change in the creature's habits, we'll have to wait forty years to find out."

ABOUT THE AUTHORS

Steve Oden has worked in the publishing industry—mainly newspapers and magazines—for more than 30 years. Although retired, he provides editorial services on a consulting basis, mainly to corporate clients, and writes on assignment. His newspaper columns have appeared regularly in Tennessee and Alabama publications since 1980, winning awards from the Alabama Press Association, University of Tennessee-Tennessee Press Association, Society of Professional Journalists, National Rural Electric Cooperative Association and several wildlife conservation organizations.

Ernie Howard was born on January 29,1977 during a Minnesota blizzard. His two story telling parents almost didn't make it to the hospital in their beat up blue Cadillac. Ernie is the writer of *Write Something!,* a book about the illusion of Writers Block. *A World Without*, a Science Fiction book about the love between a husband and wife, and the darkness that can come into a marriage. *Walter*, A Science Fiction book about a boy who is an outcast who makes a friend with a man that speaks to him through his television. Ernie lives with his wife and 3 boys in Henderson, NV, where he dreams up new stories, and tries to live everyday to the fullest.

Paul B. Kohler is the International Bestselling author of the highly acclaimed novel *Linear Shift*. His recent work includes *Turn, Detour, and Reversion*, from *The Humanity's Edge Trilogy*, along with several short stories. His short story, *Rememorations*, was included in *The Immortality Chronicles* - The Best Anthology of the Year as voted in the 2016 Predators and Editors Readers Poll. *Rememorations* was also nominated for Best American Science Fiction.

Visit Paul's main site paulkohler.net for news and updates

Jessica West (a.k.a. West1Jess) is currently pursuing a state of self-induced psychosis, also known as writing. In the past, she has worked for Wal-Mart, a lawyer, and a bank. Now if she could just get a couple years experience with the IRS and the NSA, world domination is in the bag.

Jess lives in Acadiana with three daughters still young enough to think she's cool and a husband who knows better but likes her anyway.

For news and updates visit west1jess.com

Daniel Arthur Smith is a USA Today bestselling author. His titles include *Spectral Shift, Hugh Howey Lives, The Cathari Treasure, The Somali Deception*, and a few other novels and short stories. He also curates the phenomenal short fiction series *Tales from the Canyons of the Damned* and *Frontiers of Speculative Fiction*.

He was raised in Michigan and graduated from Western Michigan University where he studied philosophy, with focus on cognitive science, meta-physics, and comparative religion. He began his career as a bartender, barista, poetry house proprietor, teacher, and then became a technologist and futurist for the Fortune 100 across the Americas and Europe.

Daniel has traveled to over 300 cities in 22 countries, residing in Los Angeles, Kalamazoo, Prague, Crete, and now writes in Manhattan where he lives with his wife and young sons.

For news and updates visit danielarthursmith.com